The Forgotten
Raincoat Mystery

Elaine Pageler

High Noon Books
Novato, California

Cover Design and Interior Illustrations: Tina Cash

International Standard Book Number: 1-57128-064-2

0 9 8 7 6 5 4 3 2 1
2 1 0 9 8 7 6 5 4 3

You'll enjoy all the High Noon Books. Write for
a free full list of titles.

Contents

CHAPTER 1

The Raincoat

The newsroom had a big clock on the wall. Brad glanced at it and jumped up. This was his lunch hour. So it was time to go.

Brad headed for the door. He took his camera. Maybe he could take some pictures along the way.

"Are you going to lunch?" Meg called after him.

Brad shook his head. "No, I'm going to the barber shop. My hair needs cutting," he said.

"Take your raincoat. It's going to rain," Meg told him.

Brad stopped at the window and looked out. "The sun is coming out," he said.

"No, it's going to rain," Meg said.

Brad went back and put on his raincoat. That was easier. He and Meg fought over their stories each day. Why fight about rain?

Nick's Barber Shop was two blocks away. It was a short walk. But the sun came out. Brad's face turned red. He was too hot in his raincoat. Why had he listened to Meg?

Another raincoat hung in the Barber Shop. It was about the same color as Brad's. He hung his next to it. But he kept his camera.

A man sat in one of the chairs. He had a cloth over his face.

Nick pointed to the other chair. "Sit down, Brad. This man's beard needs to soak for awhile. So I'll cut your hair. What have you been doing?" he asked.

"Working," Brad told him.

Nick put a cloth around Brad's neck. "I like to read the Riddle Street stories. You and Meg Green do a good job," he said.

Another man came in while Nick worked. But Brad didn't turn to see who it was.

The haircut didn't take long. Brad paid Nick and walked toward the door. The new man sat there. He read a paper. It wasn't in English.

3

"CRASH!" came a sound from outside.

Brad dashed out of the barber shop. The crash was at the end of the block. Two trucks had run into each other. One carried sand. The other had apples. Riddle Street was a mess of tan and red.

That would make a good photo. The News might use it on the front page. Brad began to take pictures.

"CRASH!" came another sound. This time it was thunder. Rain poured down.

Brad wished he had his raincoat. Then he remembered. It was still in the barber shop.

A crowd gathered. Meg was among them. "Where's your raincoat?" she called.

4

"It's in the barber shop. I need to take photos. Would you get it for me?" Brad asked.

"Sure," Meg said.

She hurried down the street. Soon she came back. The brown raincoat was in her hands.

Brad was wet by now. Water dripped off his nose. He pushed his camera and film in the pocket of the raincoat. Then he put it on. The sleeves hung two inches below his fingers.

"This isn't my raincoat. It's too big. You brought the wrong one," Brad told Meg.

They ran to Nick's. The two men were still there. So were two brown raincoats. One was Brad's. He pulled his things from the pocket of the wrong one and put them in his raincoat.

Nick looked up. "What's wrong?" he asked.

"Meg took the wrong raincoat. So we brought it back and got the right one," Brad told him.

They walked to the News. Brad emptied his raincoat pocket on the desk. Out came his camera, film, and a small red notebook.

"This notebook isn't mine. It must have been in the other raincoat. I'll take it back. It belongs to one of the men at the barber shop," Brad told her.

"He must be gone by now," Meg said.

She looked over his shoulder as he flipped through the notebook. There were only two small lines of writing in it. Who would want that?

Brad turned and tossed it in the trash.

CHAPTER 2

A Break-In

Brad's aunt and uncle had asked him to dinner. So Brad left the News early. He needed to stop at the store. His aunt wanted some things.

Halfway there, Brad saw a blue car. It seemed to be following him. He drove on to the store. Even inside, he felt as if someone were watching him.

Brad bought his things and went back out. The blue car was parked across the street. He started driving. The blue car did, too.

Yes, the car must be following him. Brad tried to see the driver's face. But the car stayed too far back.

Brad bit his lip. What should he do? His apartment house was up ahead. He pulled to a stop. Would the blue car stop, too? If so, he'd start up and drive to the police station.

But the blue car didn't stop. It zoomed on by.

Now Brad felt silly. The blue car wasn't following him. The person just needed to stop at the store.

Brad went inside and changed clothes. The storm clouds were gone now. So he hung his raincoat in the closet.

No blue car followed him to his aunt and

uncle's house. Nor did one follow him home later that night.

Brad came back to his apartment house at about 9 o'clock. He got out of his car and walked to his door. It was open! Something was wrong! He always locked his door.

The light switch was just inside. Brad reached in and snapped it on. No one was in there. But his apartment was a mess.

His raincoat and clothes had been pulled out of the closet. They lay on the floor. All the drawers of his desk had been emptied, too.

Brad reached for the phone. He called Sergeant Ward.

The policeman came fast. Sergeant Ward

His raincoat and clothes lay on the floor.
All the desk drawers had been emptied, too.

looked at the floor. "What was stolen?" he asked.

"That's what's so strange. I can't find a thing missing," Brad told him.

Sergeant Ward frowned. "There's a reason for the break-in. Some person really searched this place. Are you and Meg working on a new story?" he asked.

Brad shook his head.

"The person wants something. He must think you have it. So be careful. Call me if you need help," Sergeant Ward told him.

Brad watched the policeman leave. Then the little red notebook crossed his mind. But who would break in to get that?

Picking up all the things wasn't easy. Brad thought about the red notebook as he worked. He hadn't read what was inside. Did Meg? Brad glanced at his watch. She should still be up.

Meg was surprised to hear his voice. But she seemed pleased. "What's up?" she asked.

Brad told her about the break-in. "Perhaps the person was after that red notebook. Do you recall what was written inside?" he asked.

"No, I don't," Meg told him.

"I was afraid of that," Brad said.

"But the good news is I always need notebooks. So I took it out of the trash. It's in my desk at the News. We'll read it tomorrow," she told him.

CHAPTER 3

The Red Notebook

Brad rushed to the News early the next morning. It was only 6 o'clock. Meg was there. She gave him the notebook.

Brad looked at it. All the pages were blank except the last one. Here someone had written on two of the lines.

$$MWO - 0813$$
$$1MH - 1118$$

Meg frowned. "I guess that's two phone numbers. What do you think?" she asked.

"They could be. Phone numbers have seven digits. Letters can be used for the first three numbers," Brad said.

"Are you sure the break-in was for this notebook?" Meg asked.

"No, but the person didn't take a thing. Why else did he break in? Also I thought a car was trailing me," Brad said.

Meg frowned. "Let's find out who these phone numbers belong to," she said.

"Hello," called a voice. A man walked toward them. He wore jogging clothes. His eyes were on the notebook in Brad's hand.

Brad put it away quickly. But he knew the man had seen it.

The man held out his hand. "I'm Tab Cotter. Didn't you take pictures of the crash on Riddle Street yesterday?" he asked.

"That's right," Brad told him.

"Someone put a dent in my car yesterday. It was parked on Riddle Street. I thought it might have been caused by the crash. Your pictures could show something. May I see them?" he asked.

Brad's pictures were in his drawer. He took them out and spread them across his desk.

Tab looked at them. "I don't see my car. Thanks anyhow," he said.

Meg watched him walk away. "He really came early," she said.

"Maybe Tab was after the notebook. He

15

gave it a good look," Brad told her.

"I saw that, too," Meg said.

Brad picked up the phone. He dialed the first number. It rang twice. Then the phone girl came on. She said it wasn't a Star City number. He would need the area code. The same thing happened with the next number.

"Let me copy those. I'll phone all the area codes in our state," Meg told him.

Brad handed the notebook to her. "There's another way to check this out. Two men were in Nick's. The raincoat must belong to one of them. Nick lives above his shop. I'll go see him now," he said.

Meg was done with the numbers. So he

slipped the notebook in his pocket and left.

Brad knocked on Nick's door. He thought that would wake Nick. But the barber was already dressed.

"What's wrong? Did you lose your raincoat again?" he asked.

Brad shook his head. "There were two men here yesterday. What were their names?" he asked.

"I don't know the last man. He just came in from the street. But the first man comes here all the time. His name is Tab Cotter," Nick told him.

"Tab Cotter!" Brad exclaimed. That was the man at the News this morning.

Nick pointed to the drug store down the street. "Tab owns it. Why are you here so early? Is anything wrong?" he wanted to know.

Brad told him about the notebook and his apartment break-in. "I don't know if the two go together. But it seems strange," he said.

"What was in the notebook?" Nick asked.

"Just two phone numbers," Brad said.

He would have talked more. But he spotted Tab Cotter. The man had parked his car in front of his drug store. Now he walked inside. This was Brad's chance to check the car. Maybe it didn't have a dent.

"I'll talk to you later, Nick," Brad said. He headed out the door.

CHAPTER 4

Brad Gets Mugged

Tab's car didn't have a dent. Brad walked around it to be sure. It didn't have a scratch.

Brad started back toward the News. Perhaps Meg had luck with the phone numbers.

Two kids came toward him on skateboards. They came fast. Brad looked at them again. Both of them had caps pulled low on their faces. They wore dark glasses, too. Still Brad could see they weren't kids at all. These were men. And they came straight at him.

Brad tried to dodge them. But they crashed into him hard. Down he went.

The bump knocked Brad out for a minute. When he came to, the men were dragging him into the alley. Brad thought fast. He couldn't get away. So it was best to pretend to be knocked out. Maybe he could learn something.

The men rolled him over. They went through his pockets. One man pulled out the notebook. "Here it is. The boss will be glad to get this. He didn't know where or when to send us for the pick up," he said.

The other man spoke up. "This is the big one. Isn't it?" he asked.

"Yeah, we'll do the same as with the

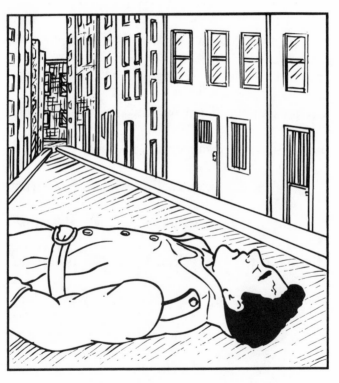

Brad heard their footsteps fade away.

others. You and I will drive the big one back to the boss's place. Now let's get out of here before someone sees us," the first man said.

Brad heard their footsteps fade away. At last it seemed safe. He opened his eyes and started to stand up. Things began to spin. Brad sat back down. Then he saw the blood on his hands. It came from a cut on his face.

At last the dizzy feeling passed. Brad tried to stand up again. He moved slowly this time. His knees felt shaky. But he limped out of the alley. The parking lot for the News was a block away. His car had a phone inside. All he had to do was get there.

The block seemed like miles. At last Brad

reached his car. He crawled inside and phoned Meg. "Come down to my car. It's in the parking lot," he said.

Minutes later, Meg opened the door to his car. "Brad! What happened to you?" she gasped.

"I got mugged. They took the notebook," he told her.

Meg crawled in beside him. She wiped away some of the blood. She was very tender.

Brad leaned against her. "Two men on skateboards knocked me out. They pulled me into an alley," he said.

"Shhh, don't talk now. Where are your keys?" Meg asked.

Brad handed them to her. "Drive me to my

apartment. I need to change clothes. Then we'll go see Sergeant Ward," Brad said.

"Forget your apartment. We're on our way to the hospital," Meg told him.

"I don't need a hospital," Brad said.

"Yes, you do. That cut needs stitches. I'll phone Sergeant Ward. He can meet us there," she told him.

"I don't need stitches," Brad started to say.

"Please don't argue," Meg snapped.

Then she reached over and touched his cheek. "I'm sorry. You took a bad blow. Let's make sure you're all right. We're up against some really bad people this time," she said.

CHAPTER 5

Talking It Over

Brad's head needed six stitches. That stopped the bleeding. There were bruises on his arms and legs, too.

The doctor also gave Brad a pill. "This will take away pain. Don't drive. Let your girlfriend do that," he said.

"She's not my girlfriend. I just work with Meg," Brad told him.

The doctor smiled. "Here's clean clothes. She got them from your apartment," he said.

Brad put them on. He threw away his old clothes. They were ripped and torn.

Meg and Sergeant Ward waited for him in the lobby. They smiled when he came out.

"Thanks for the clothes," Brad told Meg.

She grinned. "I kept trying keys from your key ring. At last one fit your door," she said.

Sergeant Ward put his hand on Brad's shoulder. "You look pale. There's a cafe here. Let's get some coffee," he said.

That sounded good to Brad. So they went to the cafe.

"Meg told me about the notebook. She says two men were in the barber shop. Tell me more about that day," Sergeant Ward said.

"O.K. I walked in the barber shop. One raincoat hung there. I put mine beside it. A man sat in the barber chair. It was Tab Cotter," Brad told them.

"Tab Cotter! Isn't that the same man who was at the News?" Meg asked.

Brad nodded. "He owns a drug store. It's up the street from Nick's Barber Shop. I saw him park his car today. It didn't have a dent," he told them.

"So Tab Cotter was in the barber's chair. What happened next?" Sergeant Ward asked.

"Tab's beard was soaking. So Nick cut my hair. Then the other man came in," Brad said.

"What's his name?" Sergeant Ward asked.

"I asked Nick. But he didn't know him. And I never saw his face. The paper was in front of it," Brad said.

"Was he reading the News?" Meg asked.

Brad shook his head. "The crash happened then. So I didn't get a good look. But it wasn't the News. I don't think it was written in English," he said.

Sergeant Ward's eyes widened at that. "Nick wouldn't have that kind of paper. The man must have brought it with him. What was the man wearing?" he asked.

"He had a raincoat. I know because there were two when we came back. Also, he was wearing a heavy sweater," Brad said.

"That's odd. It's August. The only cool place is on the ocean," Sergeant Ward said.

"Maybe he's a sailor from another country. That's why he had that paper," Meg told them.

Sergeant Ward nodded. "That could be. One of those men had the notebook. We have to find out which one," he said.

"I have another idea. The men who mugged me were talking. Their boss needs the notebook. It told where and when to pick up the big one. That means the boss had never read it. This is what I think. The two men planned to be in the barber shop at the same time. The sailor left the notebook in Tab's raincoat," Brad said.

"No one would see them talking," Meg said.

Sergeant Ward agreed again. "It sounds like we have a band of smugglers. Some big shipment is coming in the country. Do you have a copy of the note?" he asked.

Meg handed him a copy. "We thought it was two phone numbers.But I tried lots of area codes. No one answers," he said.

Sergeant Ward looked at it, too. "This must be in code. My men will work on it. I'll check out Tab Cotter, too. Now, stay out of trouble, Brad," he said.

Brad grinned. "I'll try," he told him.

CHAPTER 6

Following the Note

Brad thought of the pain pill he had taken. "I can't drive," he told Meg.

"I'll drive you. Shall we go back to the News?" she asked.

Brad nodded. "Drive up Riddle Street. I'll show you where I was mugged," he told her.

Meg drove slowly. They drove past Tab's drug store. Now they were even with Nick's Barber Shop.

"Park here," Brad told her.

They got out and walked up the block. Then Brad spotted the alley. It was a narrow walkway between two tall buildings.

Meg trembled. "Let's not go back in there," she said.

Brad didn't want to either. So they walked back to the car.

"Oh, Brad," called a voice.

Nick stood in his doorway. "I heard you were mugged. Are you all right?" he asked.

"I just have a cut on my face. Where did you hear about it?" Brad wanted to know.

"Tab told me," Nick told him.

Brad and Meg glanced at each other. Then they got back in the car.

"Sure Tab knew about it. He must have sent those men to get you. I wish we knew what that note meant," Meg said.

Brad reached for the copy of the notebook message. "Highway One," he read.

"Meg you copied the note wrong," he grumbled.

Meg snatched it out of his hand. "No, I didn't. You just had it upside down," she said.

"But it said Highway One," Brad said.

He and Meg stared at the note again. This time they read it upside down.

It read:

8||| - HW|
ε|8ο - ΟΜW

"All we had to do was turn the notebook upside down. Highway One is a place. The numbers must tell the time," Brad said.

Meg nodded. "The 8 could mean August. Today is the first of August," she told him.

"And the rest could be day 11 at 1 o'clock. Or it could say day 1 at 11 o'clock. Hey, that's today," he said.

Meg looked at the car's clock. "And it's 10 o'clock. That means the big shipment will happen in an hour," she added.

Brad shook his head. "It must mean 11 P.M. Smugglers work in the dark. They can't be seen," he said.

"What does E180-OMW mean?" Meg asked.

"Highway One is very long. It goes all the way up the coast. That must tell where to stop," he told her.

"A map might help," Meg said.

"I don't have a good one. It's a nice day for a drive. Let's go up the coast. We can figure this out. Then Sergeant Ward can be waiting for them at 11 o'clock tonight. Do you mind driving?" he asked.

Meg's eyes sparkled. "It would be fun. Do you feel well enough?" she wanted to know.

"I feel great," Brad told her.

Meg started the car and drove down Riddle Street. Soon she turned off. This road took her to Highway One.

Now they drove north. The ocean was on the left. Hills and big trees were on the right. They passed a small road. It led down to the beach.

"Exit 154," Brad read.

He glanced at the message again. "That's it. The E stands for Exit. Now we need Exit 180. So keep driving," he said.

Meg drove on. The shoreline became rougher. Lots of rocks stuck up out of the water.

"Landing a boat here would be hard. I wouldn't want to do it at night," Brad said.

There were few cars on the road. But now a gray truck roared up behind them. Two men sat inside. The driver honked the horn.

"I'm going the speed limit," Meg said.

The driver kept honking. Meg swerved out on the shoulder. The truck shot past. It skidded around the next curve.

"What a rude driver!" Brad exclaimed.

Meg turned back on the road. They drove a few miles. Then Brad saw the sign. It read:

EXIT 180

OLD MAN'S WHARF

"Oh, I've been here. Old Man's Wharf is built out into the ocean. It's old and unsafe. No one lands there anymore," Brad said.

They turned off onto the small road. It wound through the tall trees. Now they could see the small beach below. Sharp rocks were on either side.

37

Meg slammed on the brakes. "There's that gray truck. I'm not going down there," she said.

Brad saw the truck. The two men stood on the wharf. They seemed to be waving at a ship far out at sea.

His camera was on the back seat of the car. It had a long lens. That made things seem closer. Brad reached for the camera and looked at the ocean. Now he saw what the men were waving at. A fishing boat was coming in. It brought something in from that ship.

"It's 11 o'clock on August 1 at Exit 180, Old Man's Wharf. It's just as the message said. They're the smugglers and we've got to stop them," Brad told her.

The two men stood on the wharf.
They seemed to be waving at a ship.

CHAPTER 7

The Smugglers

Brad used his car phone. He called Sergeant Ward. "The boat is docking now," he said.

"Can you read its number?" Sergeant Ward wanted to know.

Brad read the number to him. "It's carrying a large box," he added.

"I'll phone the Coast Guard. They'll pick the boat up. Can you see the truck's number?" Sergeant Ward asked.

"No, I can't," Brad said.

"That's all right. We'll look for a gray truck with a large box on it. Now get out of there," Sergeant Ward said.

"We'll meet you at Tab's store. The men are going to their boss's place," Brad said.

Meg turned around and they headed back. Within a few minutes, the gray truck roared past them. It was going fast.

Sergeant Ward was at Tab's when they got there. He didn't look happy.

"The truck isn't here. We found it parked in the alley across the street. The two men were gone. We looked in the box. The top had holes and the sides were lined with foam. Nothing was in it," Sergeant Ward said.

Now Tab spoke up. "I'm not a smuggler. My car does have a dent. That's why I drove my other car today. And I don't own a raincoat," he said.

"I phoned Tab's wife. She said the same thing," Sergeant Ward told Brad and Meg.

Brad frowned. "Then who did the raincoat belong to? Wait! There was a third person in the barber shop. It was Nick," he said.

Sergeant Ward rushed to the door. "The truck was found near his shop," he said.

Nick was busy. Two men sat in the chairs. They had towels on their faces. Another man waited on the bench in the front.

"Do you own a raincoat?" Brad asked Nick.

The barber grinned. "No, I don't. Brad,

don't blame that notebook on me," he said.

"A truck is parked in the alley. Do you know anything about it?" Sergeant Ward asked.

Nick shook his head. "Lots of people park there," he said.

Meg pulled on Brad's arm. Then she pointed to the shoes of the men in the chairs.

Brad saw what she was pointing at. The men's shoes were covered with sand. "These men have been walking on the beach," he told Sergeant Ward.

The men jumped up. They rushed to the door. A policeman stopped them. He also had a fax for Sergeant Ward.

The sergeant read it. "It's from the Coast

Guard. They picked up the boat. The captain talked. They smuggle people into the United States. A sailor would come ashore. He would leave a note in Nick's raincoat. It told where to pick them up. This time it was a very rich mobster. I think that's the man sitting up front," he said.

The policeman snapped handcuffs on the man. Then he started toward Nick.

"I want a lawyer," Nick said.

Sergeant Ward turned to Brad and Meg. "The Riddle Street team has done it again. But I'm sorry that Brad got mugged," he told them.

Brad grinned at Meg. "At least I had a good nurse," he said.